Hey Diddle Diddle

Hey Diddle

Diddle

Adapted and Illustrated by
Marilyn Janovitz

Hyperion Books for Children

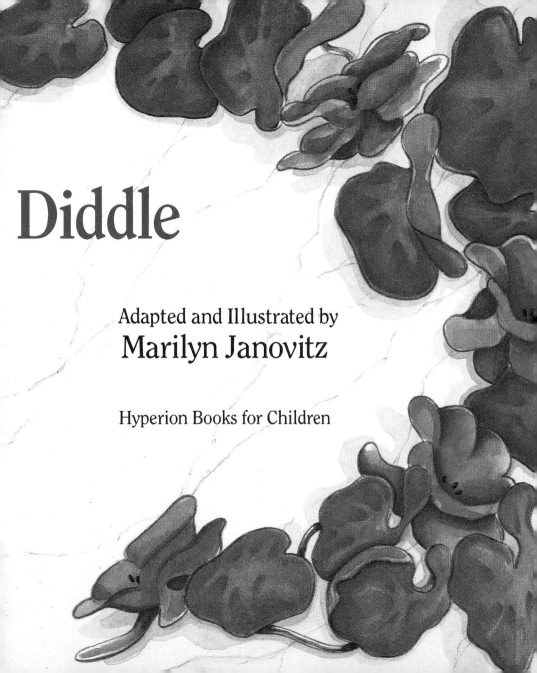

For Lydia

First Edition
1 3 5 7 9 10 8 6 4 2

Library of Congress Cataloging-in-Publication Data
Janovitz, Marilyn.
Hey diddle diddle / adapted and illustrated
by Marilyn Janovitz—1st ed.
p.   cm.
Summary: An illustrated version of the traditional nursery rhyme.
ISBN 1-56282-168-7 (trade) — ISBN 1-56282-169-5 (lib. bdg.)
1. Nursery rhymes.   2. Children's poetry.   [1. Nursery rhymes.]
I. Title.
PZ8.3.J263He   1992   398.8—dc20   91-26483   CIP   AC

The artwork for each picture consists of watercolor and colored pencil
and is prepared on Arches watercolor paper.

This book is set in 24-point ITC Clearface.

Hey diddle

diddle,

the cat and

the fiddle,

the cow jumped

over the moon.

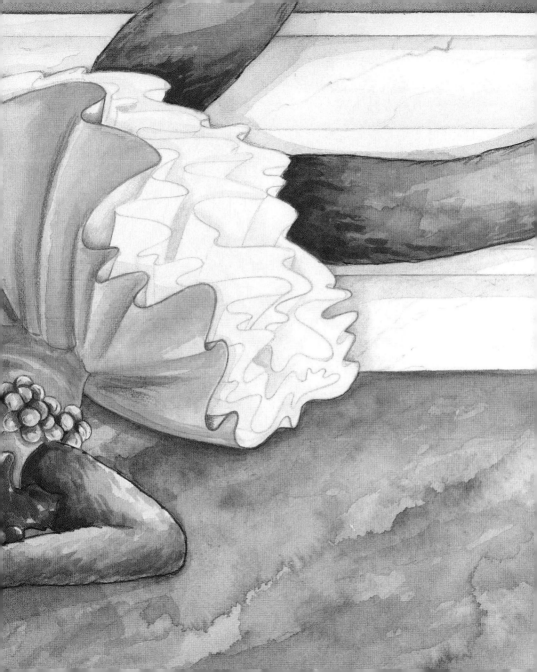

The little dog laughed

to see such a sight,

and the dish ran away

with the spoon.

Hey Did-dle Did-dle, The cat and the fid-dle, The

cow jumped o – ver the moon; _____ The

lit-tle dog laughed to see such a sight And the

dish ran a – way with the spoon.